Crusty Cupcake's Christmas Catastrophe

Sarviol Publishing
Copyright © Nick Rokicki and Joseph Kelley, 2015

ISBN: 978-1514877630

Special wholesale and re-sale rates are available. For more information,
please contact Deb Harvest at petethepopcorn@gmail.com

When purchasing this book, please consider purchasing
an additional copy to donate to your local library.

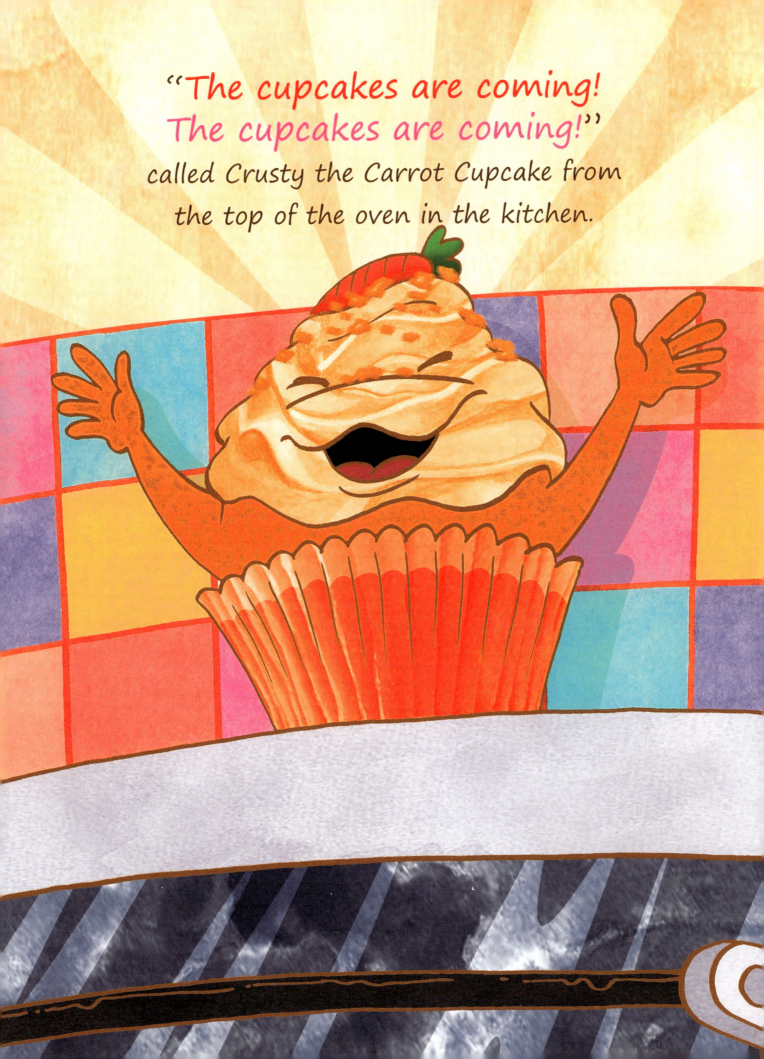

"The cupcakes are coming! The cupcakes are coming!" called Crusty the Carrot Cupcake from the top of the oven in the kitchen.

The **cupcakes** are **coming**? We're already here!'' questioned Reagan the Rainbow Cupcake, looking at all of the cupcakes surrounding her.

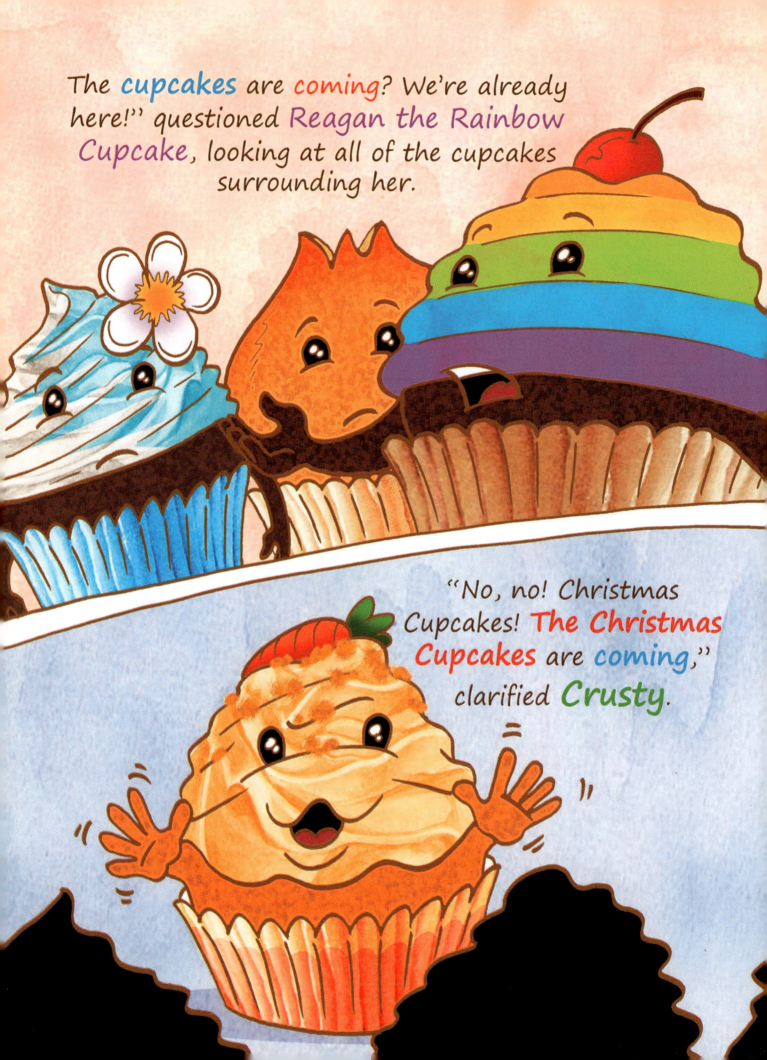

"No, no! Christmas Cupcakes! **The Christmas Cupcakes** are **coming**,'' clarified **Crusty**.

"Christmas Cupcakes? I love Christmas! And I **love** cupcakes! Put them together and that's gonna be crazy!" exclaimed Tammy the Tropical Cupcake.

"I think Christmas Cupcakes sound kinda creepy... I mean, are they gonna be shaped like giftboxes or stockings?" asked Cornelius.

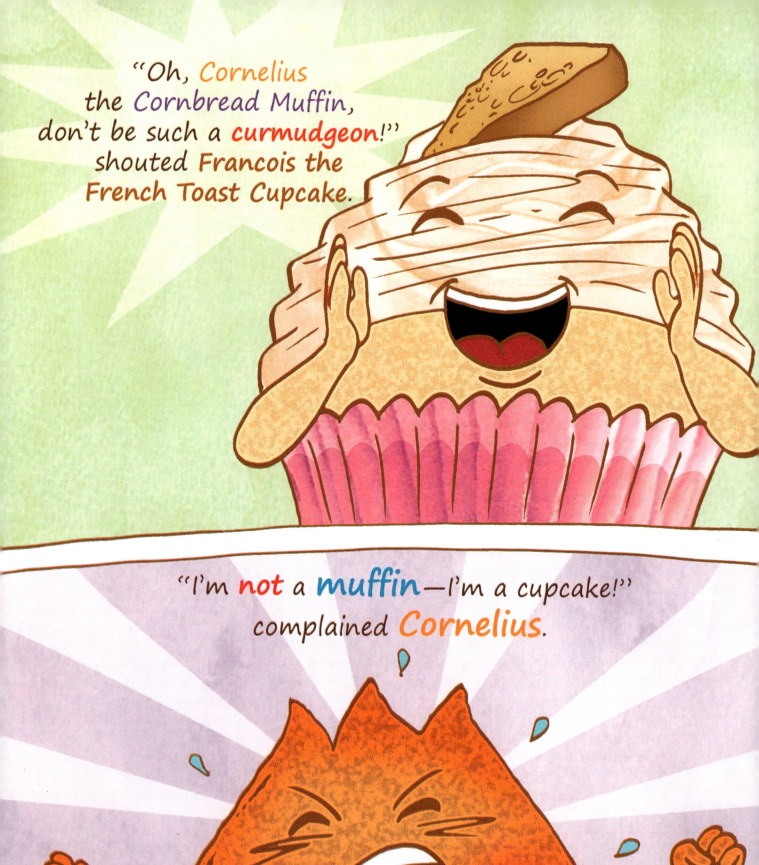

"Oh, Cornelius the Cornbread Muffin, don't be such a curmudgeon!" shouted Francois the French Toast Cupcake.

"I'm not a muffin—I'm a cupcake!" complained Cornelius.

"Whoever heard of a **cornbread cupcake?**"
teased Francois.
"I have **frosting**! That makes me a **cupcake**!"
said **Cornelius**.

"Calm! Calm!" came the voice of Crusty, the oldest cupcake at Campbell's Sweets Factory. "We have lots of work to do. I want everything to be perfect for the arrival of the Christmas Cupcakes!"

Over the **next several weeks**, Crusty came up with **chores** for each cupcake to accomplish. **Loretta the Lollipop Cupcake** was creative with her hands, so she **wrapped** the **gifts** that Crusty had purchased.

To: Pete the Popcorn
From: Panni the Popcorn

Peyton the Pineapple Cupcake was **taller** than the other cupcakes, so he was **responsible** for **placing** the **star** on top of the **Christmas tree**.

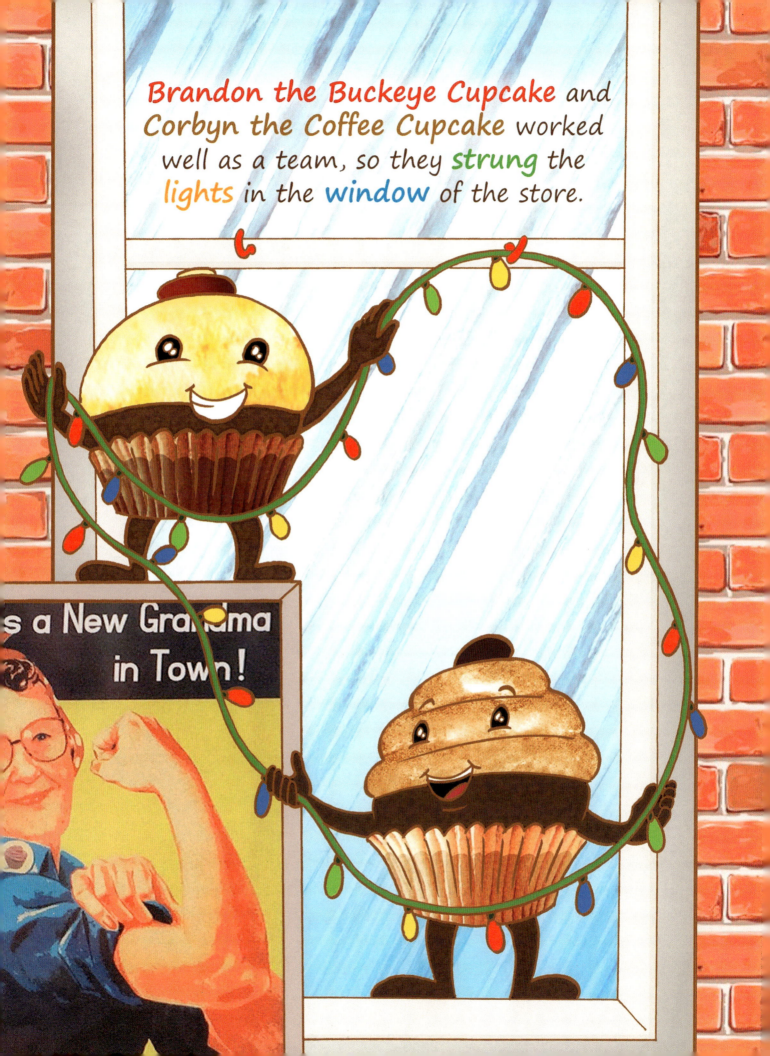

Brandon the Buckeye Cupcake and **Corbyn the Coffee Cupcake** worked well as a team, so they **strung** the **lights** in the **window** of the store.

Zack the Zucchini Cupcake was capable of climbing, so he creeped up the ladder to hang the stockings high.

Molly the Marshmallow Cupcake was the best reader at **Campbell's Sweets Factory**, so she read off the **list** of **chores** that **Crusty** had **written**.

Carlos Consuelos, CC for short, the
Cookies and Cream Cupcake, really liked
the fresh smell that comes with a clean
cupcake case, so he was the
Cleaner-in-Chief.

Freda the German Chocolate Cupcake and Amos "Jupie" the Apricot Jelly Cupcake were the best bakers at Campbell's, so they whipped up chocolate treats for dessert.

Vivian the Vanilla Cupcake was gifted with patience, so she **decorated** the **cookies** that came from the oven.

"Where is **Crusty** while we are doing all of this work?" asked **Brooklyn the Bacon Cupcake**, who was practicing her cursive as she **wrote** the **invitations**.

"A **holiday** wouldn't be a **hootenanny** without the ham," shouted **Crusty**, walking in the door to **Campbell's Sweets Factory** with the **biggest ham** any of the cupcakes had ever seen!

"Bedtime it is! The Christmas Cupcakes are coming tomorrow ... and I have to wake up early."

Sure enough, **Crusty** woke up at the crack of dawn, the smile on his face bright enough to light the kitchen. He carefully coated the ham with honey and graham crackers, delicately placing it in the oven.

Several hours passed as all the **cupcakes** ran around the shop in a **frenzy**, making final **preparations**. Suddenly, a loud beeping noise **erupted** from the kitchen. **Crusty** ran out of the swinging doors, a cloud of **smoke** behind him.

"**Fire** in the oven! **Evacuate! Don't push!**"
said **Crusty**, loud enough for everyone to hear.

Soon, a **fire truck** arrived in front of the shop, where the **cupcakes** had gathered a **safe distance** away.

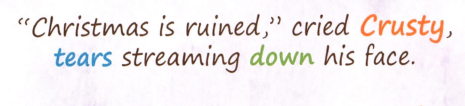

"Christmas is ruined," cried **Crusty**, **tears** streaming **down** his face.

"Calm, calm, Crusty..." said **Freda**. "Thankfully, we learned a lot when **Firefighter Stephen** visited the store to **teach** us all about **fire safety**. If he hadn't, you might not have **installed** that extra **smoke alarm**."

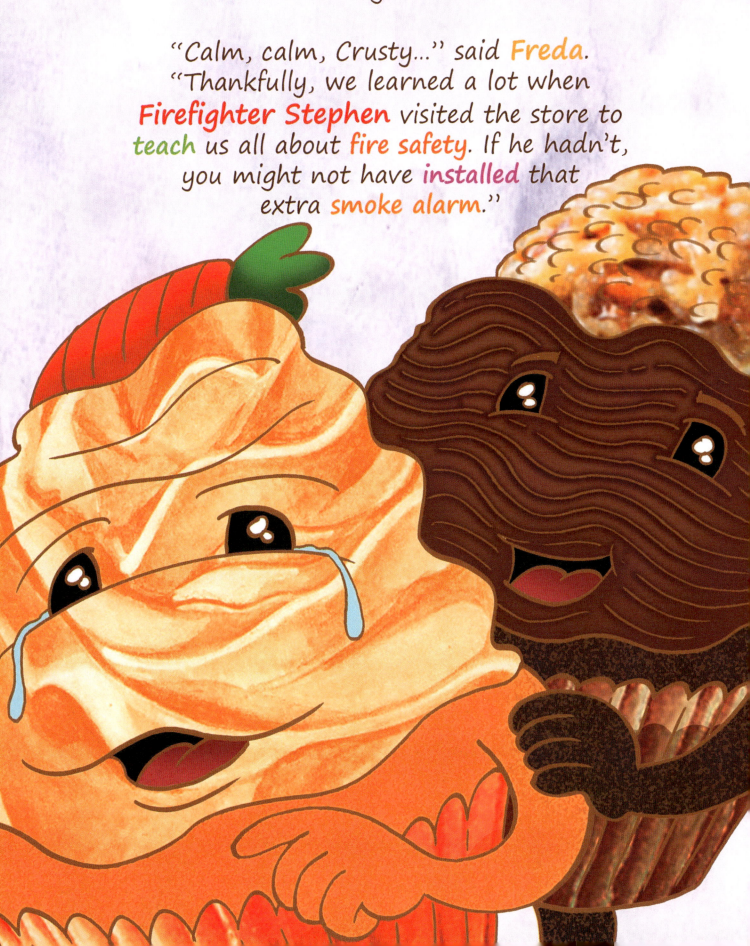

"Yeah, Crusty... Christmas isn't ruined!
I'm just happy to be here and meet a lot of new
friends," came a cheerful voice from behind.
"I'm Melissa... the Mistletoe Cupcake.
The others are on their way!"

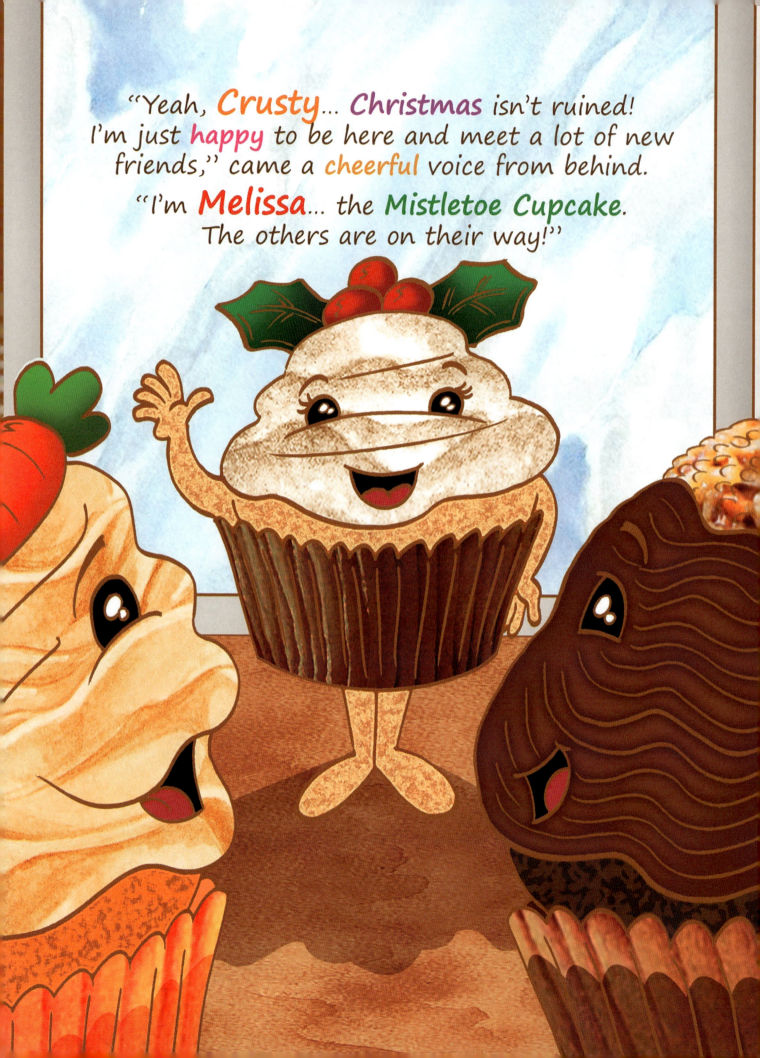

"We've got **good news**," said Firefighter Brian, walking out the door of Campbell's. "Because you used your **fire extinguisher**, the **fire** was **contained** in the oven! Outside, it was just a lot of smoke."

"So **Christmas** isn't ruined, after all?" asked **Crusty**.

"All you've **gotta** do is let the **smoke clear**... and maybe think up a new **dinner** plan, because the **ham** is a little overdone," joked **Firefighter James**.

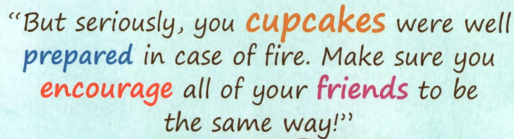

"But seriously, you **cupcakes** were well **prepared** in case of fire. Make sure you **encourage** all of your **friends** to be the same way!"

"**Cupcakes** don't eat ham, anyway," said Carlos, clapping **Crusty** on the back. "Besides, **Christmas** is a **feeling inside** of you— you can't ruin that!"

Just then, the factory's **delivery truck** pulled up.

"The **Christmas Cupcakes** are here!" **shouted** the group. Sure enough, the **beautiful** Christmas Cupcakes **filed** out of the truck and **walked** into the **shop**.

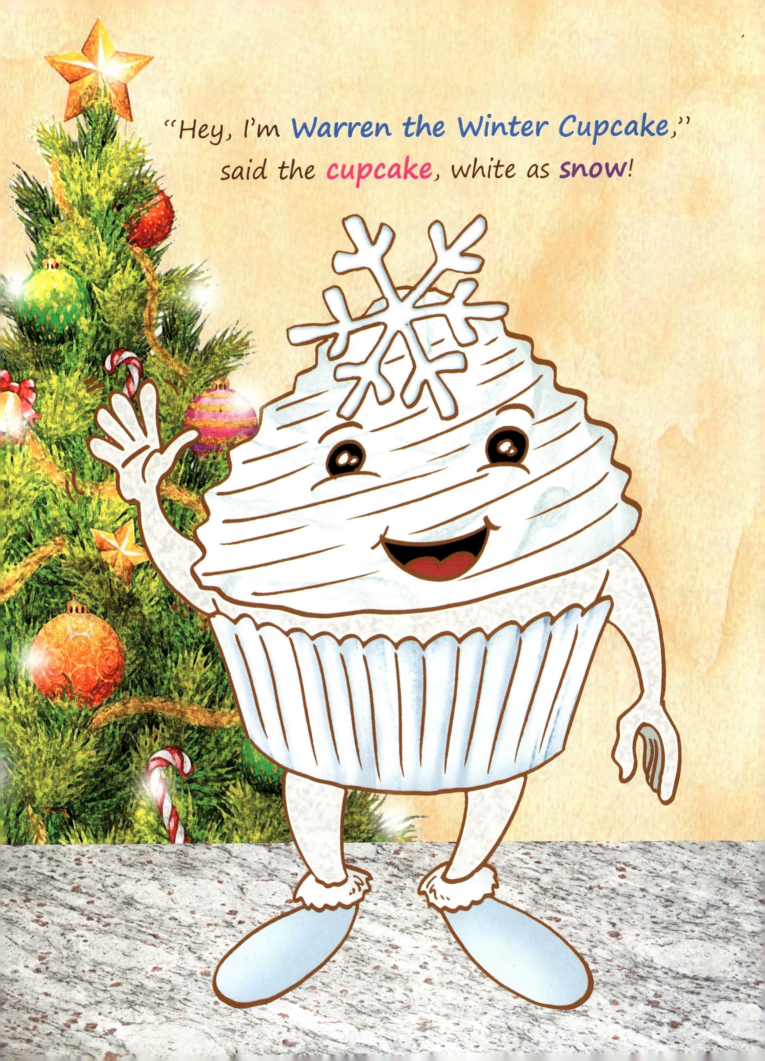

"Hey, I'm Warren the Winter Cupcake,"
said the cupcake, white as snow!

"And I'm **Rachel** the **Reindeer Cupcake!**" purred the cupcake that looked just like one of **Santa's** drivers.

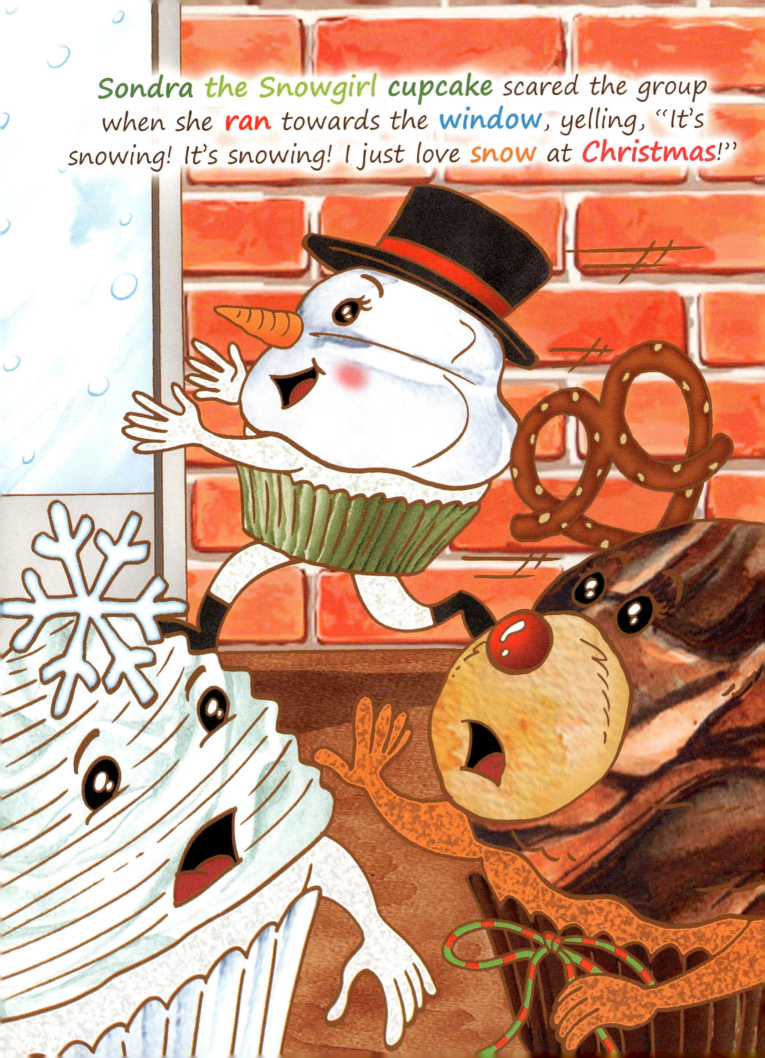

Sondra the Snowgirl cupcake scared the group when she ran towards the window, yelling, "It's snowing! It's snowing! I just love snow at Christmas!"

"I'm **thirsty**!" exclaimed Ethan the Eggnog Cupcake,
heading straight for the **bowl** of **cranberry punch**.

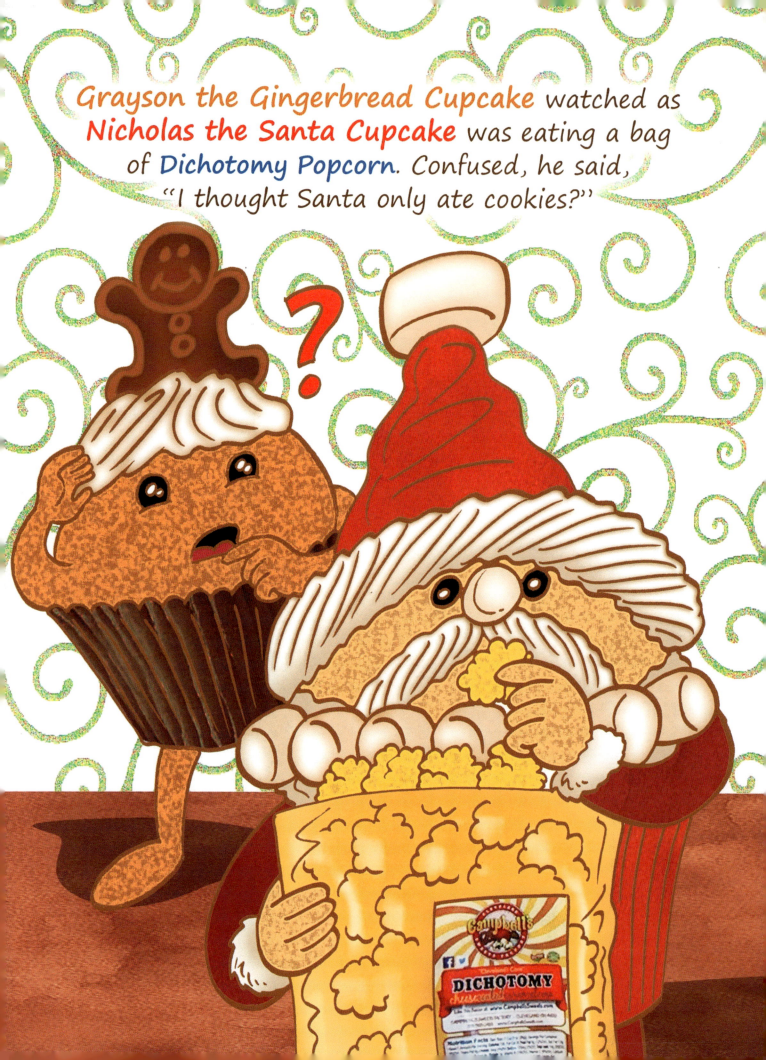

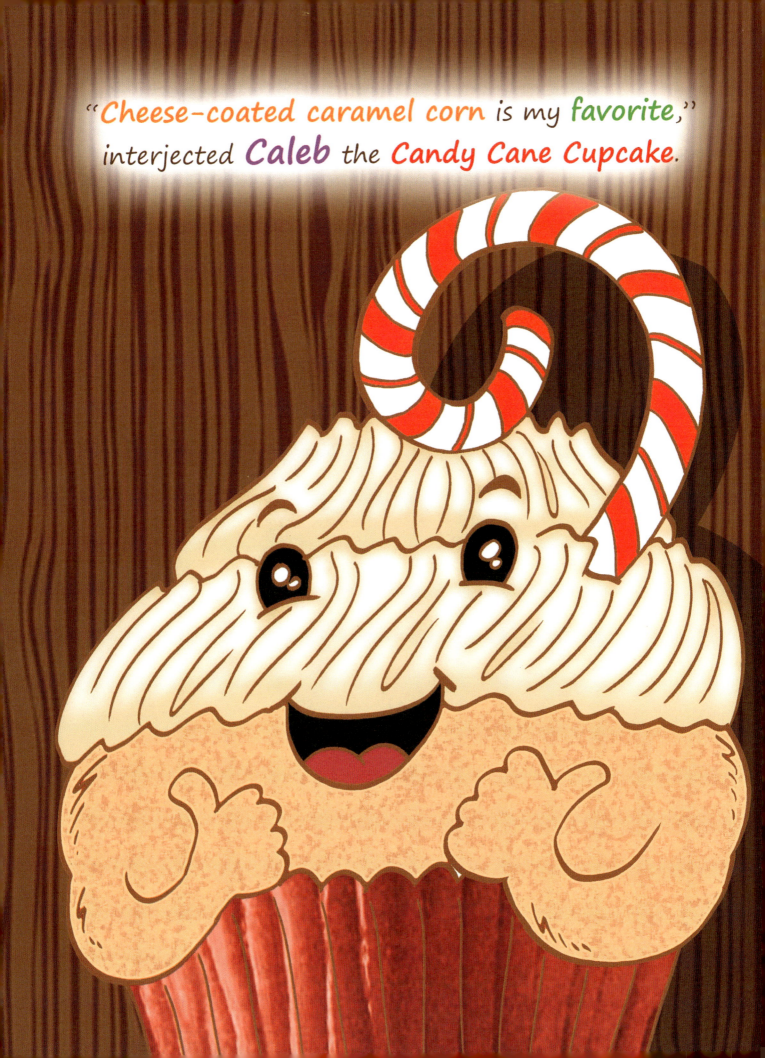

"Cheese-coated caramel corn is my *favorite*," interjected **Caleb** the **Candy Cane Cupcake**.

"All this **talk** about **food** is making me **hungry**! Have you ever tried a **cupcake** made out of **meatloaf**? With **mashed potato** frosting?" asked **Emily the Elf Cupcake**.

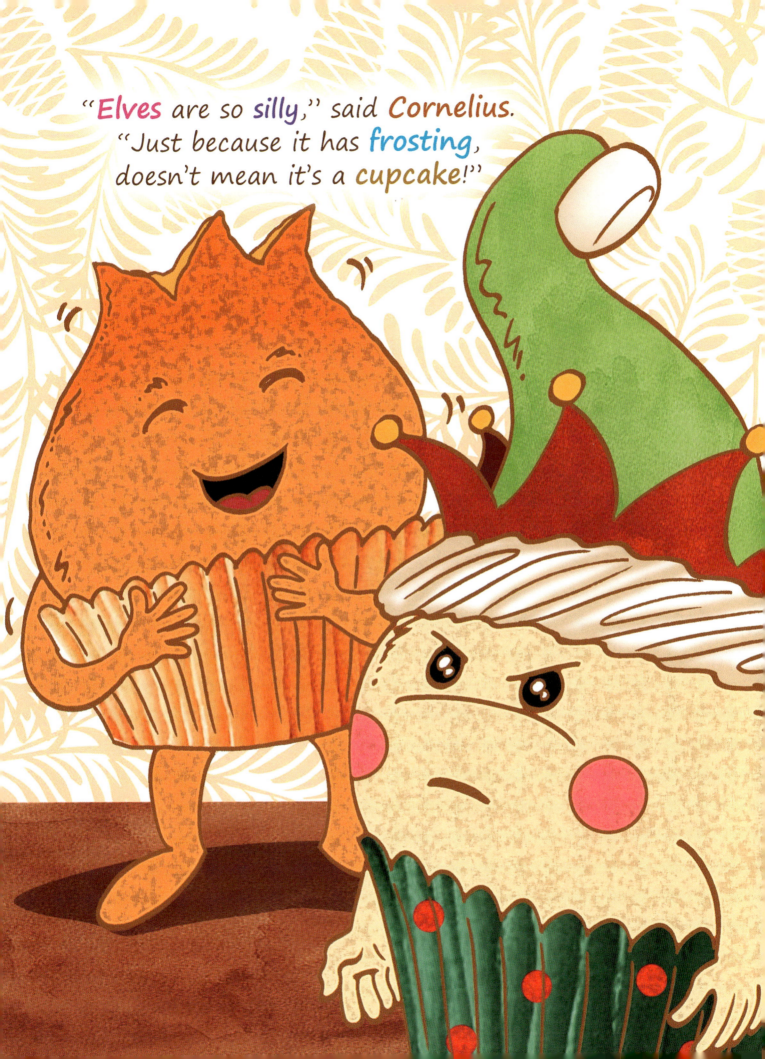

"**Elves** are so **silly**," said Cornelius. "Just because it has **frosting**, doesn't mean it's a **cupcake**!"

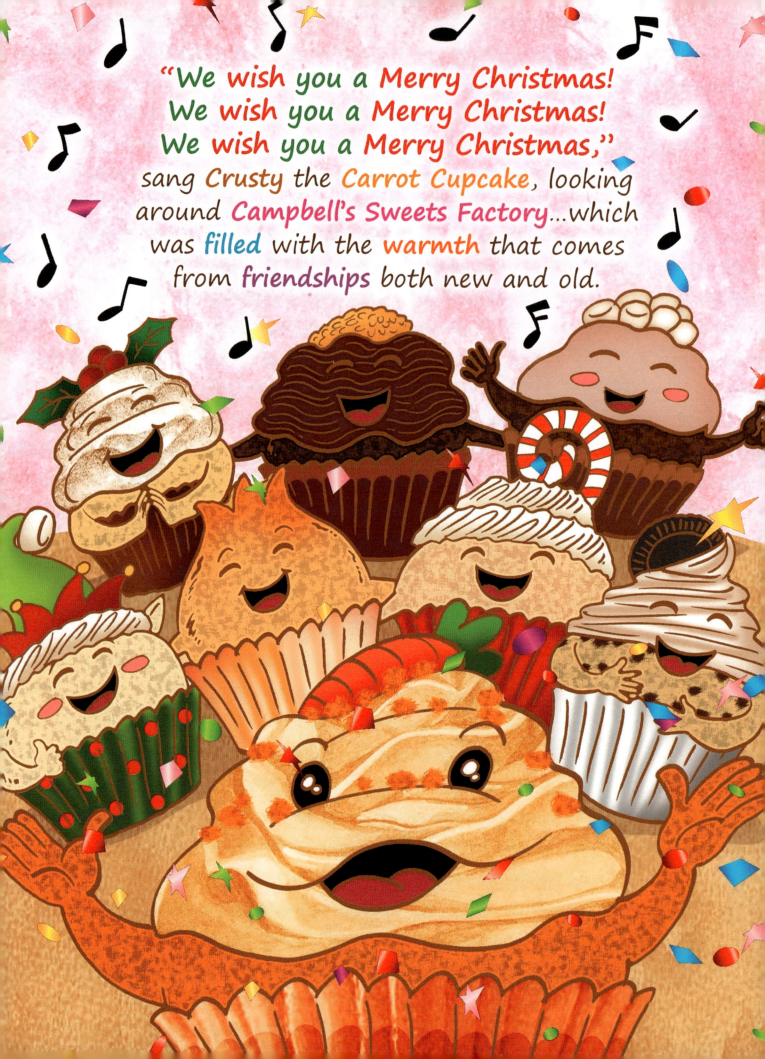

"We wish you a Merry Christmas!
We wish you a Merry Christmas!
We wish you a Merry Christmas,"
sang Crusty the Carrot Cupcake, looking
around Campbell's Sweets Factory...which
was filled with the warmth that comes
from friendships both new and old.

Campbell's Sweets heritage spans four decades of candy-making excellence, beginning with our father Amos "Jupie" Campbell and his famous Karmelkorn.®

Our current journey began in 2004 with the opening of Campbell's Popcorn Shop in Cleveland's historic West Side Market. A few years later, the operation was expanded to another stand in the market, where we offered Grandma Freda Campbell's Cupcakes!

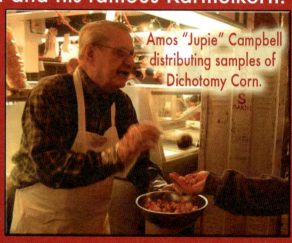

Amos "Jupie" Campbell distributing samples of Dichotomy Corn.

Grandma Campbell's smiling face on our cupcake boxes!

In 2011, with demand exploding, we opened Campbell's Sweets Factory in Ohio City. Then, in 2013, we further expanded by opening another factory location in Lakewood, Ohio. We are still growing— with products being sold at several retail locations and even online at www.CampbellsSweets.com

Campbell's Sweets Factory
CLEVELAND
2084 W. 25th Street
Cleveland, Ohio 44113

Campbell's Popcorn Shop
WEST SIDE MARKET
1979 W. 25th Street
Cleveland, Ohio 44113

Campbell's Sweets Factory
LAKEWOOD
14730 Detroit Avenue
Lakwood, Ohio 44107

www.CampbellsSweets.com

A Note From Joe and Nick...

This is our 12th published book for children. Honestly, it's a little hard to believe. The journey has been wonderful. From school visits to festivals... from libraries to family reading nights... from working with businesses all over the country... to reading our books right in your living room, surrounded by friends and family that take a true interest in the creativity of a child. This journey wouldn't have been started without the solid base of education that was instilled in us by our parents. So, in this Christmas-themed book, we included a special honor. Sondra, the Snowgirl Cupcake, is Joe's Mother. And Noel the Cupcake is a shout-out to Nick's father, Leon. The respect for reading and learning that they gave us will never be forgotten.

Joe Kelley, with his Mom Sondra.

Nick Rokicki, with his Dad Leon.

A Note From Ronaldo Florendo...

I would first like to thank Nick and Joe for this awesome ride. I enjoy doing your cute stories and characters. I would also like to thank the people who continuously support the books we are doing. You're an amazing inspiration and please continue reading... don't miss our upcoming books. Cheers and Merry Christmas - Ron

Made in the USA
Charleston, SC
13 November 2015